How and Why
Folktales

From Around the World

Arlene Egelberg
Raymond C. Clark

with Illustrations by Chuck Braun

PRO LINGUA  ASSOCIATES

Pro Lingua Associates, Publishers
P.O. Box 1348
Brattleboro, Vermont 05302 USA
Office: 802 257 7779
Orders: 800 366 4775
Email: info@ProLinguaAssociates.com
WebStore www.ProLinguaAssociates.com
SAN: 216-0579

At ***Pro Lingua***
our objective is to foster an approach
to learning and teaching that we call
***interplay**, the **inter**action of language*
learners and teachers with their materials,
with the language and culture,
and with each other in active, creative,
*and productive **play**.*

Copyright © 2004 by Arlene Egelberg

ISBN 0-86647-180-4

The sources for these stories are listed on page 98. The world map on page vi is an outline mercator projection available for free with hundreds of other maps at WorldAtlas.com. Copyright © 1996-2004 Graphic Maps, a d/b/a of the Woolwine/Moen Group.

This book was designed by Arthur A. Burrows and set in Bookman Oldstyle, a modern, bold adaptation of a traditional square serif face, with Arab Brushstroke, a calligraphic display face; these are both Agfa digital fonts. The book was printed and bound by Boyd Printing Company in Albany, New York.

Printed in the United States of America
First printing 2004.
There are 2000 copies in print.

Contents

Introduction

Long ago, all around the world, before television and even before books, the people of the world told stories for entertainment and instruction. One favorite kind of story was told to explain the marvelous and mysterious world they lived in. We can easily imagine that, just as children of today still ask "why" and "how," the children of long ago asked these same questions, and adults created imaginative and dramatic stories to tell and pass down to the next generation.

This collection of stories from eleven different cultures is simply a sampling of the creativity of the human mind. In this book, we present them for entertainment and instruction, and we hope you will enjoy them, learn, and appreciate the diversity of the world we live in.

The stories are suitable for high beginner and intermediate learners of English. Although the stories are very suitable for upper elementary school students, grades four and above, they work equally well with young adult and adult students. Each story has a variety of exercises that allow for work in all four skill areas (reading, writing, listening, speaking), as well as activities focused on lexical and grammatical matters. They progress in length and complexity from the first story to the last. For that reason, it is best to begin at the beginning and proceed in order through the book.

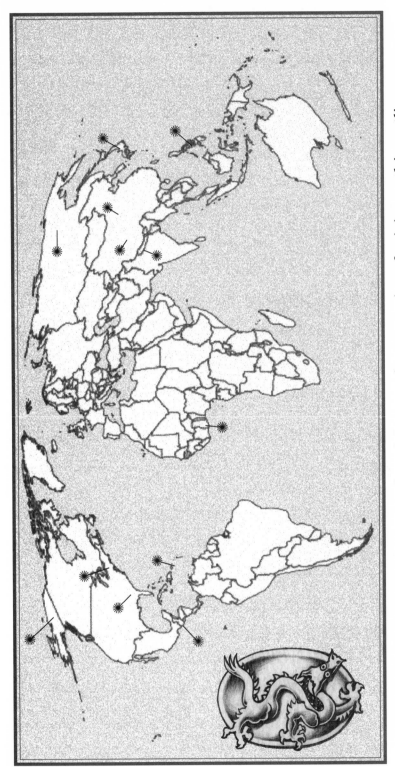

Where do these folktales come from? Locate the countries of origin on this outline map.

Why the Sky Is High

The Philippines

Discuss.

Do you know these words?

sky, stick, prayer, feast, dance, spear

Read.

Many years ago the world was new. The **sky** was very low. People could touch it with a **stick**. God answered their **prayers** quickly. But people did not behave well. God was angry and made them work. Finally, He let them rest. They had a great **feast**. One of the **dancers** threw his **spear** in the air.

Answer.

1. What could people do with a stick?
2. How did God answer people's prayers?
3. How did people behave?
4. What did God make them do?
5. What did a dancer do?

Discuss.

What happened when the dancer threw his spear in the air?

1

Why the Sky Is High

Many years ago, the world was new. The sky was very low. People could touch the sky easily with a stick. God also was very close. He could hear people's prayers. He answered them quickly. People did not need to work. Life was easy.

Then everything changed. People did not behave well, and God was very angry. He did not answer their prayers, and He made them work hard.

After the people had worked for many months, God let them have some days of rest. The people had a big feast. They had a wonderful time with lots of dancing. One of the dancers forgot the sky was so close. He threw his spear in the air. It stabbed the sky and hurt an angel.

God was angry again, and He raised the sky high above the earth. And now no one can touch it.

New Words.

Look at the story again and underline the words that you are not sure of. Write them below, and then ask your classmates or teacher about them, or look them up in a dictionary.

Write T for True and F for False.

1. ___ Many years ago, life for people was easy.

2. ___ People could touch the sky.

3. ___ God was very far away.

4. ___ He couldn't answer people's prayers.

5. ___ People did not need to work.

6. ___ God became very angry when the people did not behave well.

7. ___ God told the people to pray.

8. ___ He made them work for many months.

9. ___ The people decided to dance in the sky.

10. ___ A dancer threw his spear at God.

☞ *Check your answers in the story; then write your score here and on page 97.* **Right: ____/10**

Write. Finish these sentences.

Many years ago,

Then

After

And now

4

Read, write, and look again.

Many years ago, the world was _____. The sky was very _____.

People could touch the sky _____ with a stick. God also was very

_____. He could hear people's prayers. He answered them _____.

People did not need to

work. Life was _____.

Then everything

changed. People did not

behave _____, and God

was very _____. He

did not answer their

prayers, and He made

them work _____.

After the people had

worked for _____ months,

God let them have some days of rest. The people had a _____ feast.

They had a _____ time with lots of dancing. One of the dancers

forgot the sky was so _____. He threw his spear in the air. It

stabbed the sky and hurt an angel.

God was angry again, and He raised the sky _____ above the

earth. And now no one can touch it.

Pronounce these words.

answered	touched	needed
stabbed	danced	
raised	worked	
changed		
behaved		

Use the words above in these sentences. Then say the sentences.

1. Nobody _____ to work.

2. The spear _____ the sky.

3. They _____ at the feast.

4. A person _____ the sky with a stick.

5. God _____ their prayers quickly.

6. The people _____ very badly.

7. God _____ the sky very high.

8. The people _____ hard for many months.

9. Life was easy, but then everything _____.

Write a sentence for each word.

was

were

can

could

hear

heard

have

has

had

forget

forgot

throw

threw

makes

made

lets

let

hurts

hurt

Listen to and tell the story of why the sky is high

Many years ago ......

People could ......

God also ......

People did not need ......

Then everything ......

People did not ...... ,

and God ......

After the people had worked ......

The people had ......

One of the dancers ......

It stabbed ......

God was ......

And now, ...

Put on a play

Tell the story "Why the Sky Is High" as a play.
These are the characters:

Announcer

People

God

Dancer

Angel

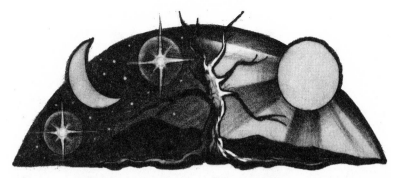

How Chipmunk Got Her Stripes

Native American Seneca

Discuss.

What do these words mean?

chipmunk, stripe, bear, darkness, light, hole

Read.

Long ago, the animals talked about day and night. **Bear** wanted **darkness** all the time. **Chipmunk** wanted day and night. They argued for a long time. Finally the sun rose. There was **light**. Chipmunk was happy. Bear was angry, and he chased chipmunk to her **hole**.

Answer.

1. What did the animals talk about?
2. What did Bear want?
3. What did Chipmunk want?
4. How long did they argue?
5. When the sun rose, how did Chipmunk feel?
6. What did Bear do?

Discuss.

What happened when Bear chased Chipmunk?

How Chipmunk Got Her Stripes

O ne time long ago, the animals had a meeting. They wanted to decide if the world should have night all the time, or if the world should have day and night.

Bear wanted night all the time. Chipmunk wanted day and night. They began to argue. "Night is best. Let us have darkness," sang the bear. Chipmunk sang, "The light will come. Let us have light."

"Night is best. Give us darkness," Bear repeated. He raised his voice because he was so sure that he was right. Chipmunk spoke louder, "The light will come. Give us light." They went on and on like this. The other animals had no chance to speak.

Finally, the sky showed its first bright red color. "Light is coming," Chipmunk sang happily. The sun rose higher and daylight filled the sky. Bear was very angry. He chased Chipmunk, but the little animal got away. She jumped into her hole in a tree, but before she got in the hole, Bear's big claws made marks on Chipmunk's back. And that is why Chipmunk has stripes today.

New Words.

Underline new words in the story. Write them below and find out their meaning.

Write T for True and F for False.

1. ___ All the animals wanted night all the time.

2. ___ Chipmunk wanted day and night.

3. ___ Chipmunk and Bear argued.

4. ___ The other animals also wanted day and night.

5. ___ Finally, the sky showed a yellow color.

6. ___ Bear chased Chipmunk.

7. ___ Chipmunk couldn't get away.

8. ___ Chipmunk jumped into a tree.

9. ___ Bear's claws made a mark on Chipmunk.

10. ___ Chipmunks have stripes on their backs.

☞ *Check your answers in the story; then write your score here and on page 97.* **Right: ____/10**

Write. Finish these sentences.

One time long ago,

Bear wanted

Chipmunk wanted

Finally, the sky

And that is why

12

Read, write, and look again.

One time _____ ago, the animals had a meeting. They wanted to decide if the world should have night _____ the time, or if the world should have day and night.

Bear wanted night _____ the time. Chipmunk wanted day and night. They began to argue. "Night is _____. Let us have darkness," sang Bear. Chipmunk sang, "The light will come. Let us have light."

"Night is _____. Give us darkness," Bear repeated. He raised his voice because he was so _____ that he was _____. Chipmunk spoke _____, "The light will come. Give us light." They went on and on like this. The other animals had no chance to speak.

Finally, the sky showed its first _____ red color. "Light is coming," Chipmunk sang _____. The sun rose _____ and daylight filled the sky. Bear was very _____. He chased Chipmunk, but the little animal got away. She jumped into her hole in a tree, but before she got in the hole, Bear's _____ claws made marks on Chipmunk's back. And that is why Chipmunk has stripes today.

Pronounce these words.

behaved	touched	needed
answered	danced	wanted
showed	worked	decided
filled	chased	repeated
argued	jumped	

Use seven of the words above in these sentences. Then say the sentences.

1. A person _____ the sky with a stick.

2. God _____ prayers quickly.

3. They _____ very badly.

4. They _____ to work again.

5. They _____ very hard.

6. Everybody _____ at the feast.

* * * * * * * * * * * * * * * *

7. Chipmunk _____ to have day and night.

8. Finally, the sky _____ its first color.

9. Bear _____ "Night is best," several times.

10. Daylight _____ the sky.

11. Bear _____ Chipmunk.

12. Chipmunk _____ into a hole.

13. Bear and Chipmunk _____ about night and day.

14. The animals _____ to have a meeting.

14

Write a sentence for each word.

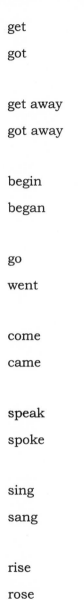

get

got

get away

got away

begin

began

go

went

come

came

speak

spoke

sing

sang

rise

rose

Listen to and tell the story of Chipmunk and Bear.

One time long ago, ...

They wanted to decide ......

Bear wanted ......

Chipmunk wanted ......

They began ....

The other animals ......

Finally, the sky......

"Light is coming," ......

The sun rose ......

Bear was ......

He chased Chipmunk, but ......

He jumped ......,

but before ......,

Bear's big claws ......

And that is why ......

 Put on a play.

Tell the story "How Chipmunk Got Her Stripes" as a play.
These are the characters:

Announcer

Some animals

Bear

Chipmunk

The sun

How the Sea Was Born

A Taino Folktale from the Caribbean

Discuss.

Do you know these words?

spirit, bones, gourd, roof, hut

Read.

The Great **Spirit**, Yaya, killed His son. He put his **bones** in a **gourd**. He hung the gourd from the **roof** of His **hut**. One day He looked in the gourd. It was full of water. There were many fish in the water. He put the gourd back. Mother Earth's son came into Yaya's hut and took the gourd down. He broke it.

Answer.

1. Who was the Great Spirit?
2. What did He do to His son?
3. What did He put in a gourd?
4. Who came into Yaya's hut?
5. Who broke the gourd?

Discuss.

What happened when Mother Earth's son broke the gourd?

How the Sea
Was Born

The Great Spirit, Yaya, had a son. His name was Yayael. When Yayael grew up he behaved very badly. He made his father angry. His father said, "Leave home at once, and do not return for four months."

Yayael returned, but still he behaved badly. One day, Yaya got very angry and killed His son. He put His son's bones in a gourd and hung it very high from the roof of His hut.

After a while, Yaya wanted to see His son again. He took the gourd down and looked inside. What a surprise! Inside the gourd there was water with many fish swimming around. The fish were different sizes, some big, some little, and they were very colorful. He put the gourd back.

Then one day, Mother Earth's son got into Yaya's hut. He sneaked in while Yaya was in His garden. He saw the gourd and took it down. When he heard Yaya returning, he tried to put the gourd back, but it crashed to the ground and broke.

All at once, the water rushed from the broken gourd and covered Mother Earth with rivers, lakes, seas, and oceans. And now Earth's waters have all kinds of fish in all the colors of the rainbow.

19

New Words.

Underline new words in the story. Write them below and find out their meaning.

Write T for True and F for False.

1. ____ Yayael was the Great Spirit.

2. ____ Yaya's son behaved very badly.

3. ____ Yaya told His son to leave the hut.

4. ____ When Yayael returned he behaved very well.

5. ____ Yaya put His son's bones in the garden.

6. ____ Yayael's bones became fish.

7. ____ The fish were small and black.

8. ____ Mother Earth sneaked into Yaya's hut.

9. ____ When the gourd broke, the water rushed out.

10. ____ All the fish went into the sea.

☞ *Check your answers in the story; then write your score here and on page 97.* **Right: ____/10**

Write. Finish these sentences.

The Great Spirit

Yayel returned

After a while

All at once

And now

20

Read, write, and look again.

The _____ Spirit, Yaya, had a son. His name was Yayael. When

Yayael grew up he behaved very _____. He made his father

_____. His father said, "Leave home at once, and do not return

for _____ months."

Yayael returned, but still he behaved _____. One day, Yaya got

very _____ and killed His son. He put His son's bones in a gourd

and hung it very _____ from the ceiling of His hut.

After a while, Yaya wanted to see

His son again. He took the gourd

_____ and looked inside. What

a surprise! _____ the gourd

there was water with many fish

swimming around. The fish were

_____ sizes, some _____,

some _____, and they were very

_____. He put the gourd back.

Then one day, Mother Earth's son got _____ Yaya's hut. He

sneaked in while Yaya was in His garden. He saw the gourd and took

it _____. When he heard Yaya returning, he tried to put the

gourd _____, but it crashed to the ground and broke.

All at once, the water rushed from the _____ gourd and covered

Mother Earth with rivers, lakes, seas and oceans. And now Earth's

waters have _____ kinds of fish in _____ the colors of the rainbow.

Pronounce these words.

showed	jumped	repeated
argued	sneaked	decided
killed	crashed	wanted
returned	rushed	
tried	looked	
covered		

Use the words above in these sentences. Then say the sentences.

1. The animals _____ to have a meeting.

2. Bear and Chipmunk _____ for a long time.

3. Bear _____ darkness all the time.

4. Bear _____ his words several times.

5. Chipmunk _____ into a hole.

6. The sky _____ a bright, red color.

　　* * * * * * * * * * * * * * *

7. Yayael _____ home after four months.

8. Mother Earth's son _____ into the hut.

9. The water _____ Mother Earth.

10. The gourd _____ to the ground and broke.

11. Yaya _____ inside the gourd.

12. The water _____ out of the gourd.

13. He _____ to put the gourd back.

14. Yaya _____ his son.

22

Write a sentence for each word.

grow up

grew up

hang

hung

leave

left

put

put

take

took

see

saw

hear

heard

break

broke

Listen to and tell the story of how the sea was born.

The great spirit, ...

When Yayael grew up ......

His father said, " ...... "

Yayael returned, ...

He put his son's bones ......

After a while, ...

He took the gourd ....

Inside the gourd ......

Then one day, Mother Earth's son ....

He saw the gourd ....

When he heard ......

All at once, the water rushed ....

And now ....

 Put on a play.

Tell the story of "How the Sea Was Born" as a play. These are the characters:

> Announcer
>
> Yaya
>
> Yayael
>
> Mother Earth
>
> Mother Earth's son

Why Birds Are
Different Colors

An African-American Folk Tale from North Carolina

Discuss.

What do these words mean?

flood, ark, sign, rainbow, hummingbird

Read.

After the great **flood**, Noah did not want the animals to leave the **ark**. He wanted a **sign** from God. God created a **rainbow**. Noah let the animals leave. The animals were very happy. The birds were especially happy. They flew into the rainbow. The **hummingbird** flew through the rainbow many times.

Answer.

1. What did Noah want from God?
2. What did God do?
3. How did the birds feel?
4. What did the birds do?
5. What did the hummingbird do?

Discuss.

What happened to the birds?

Why Birds Are
Different Colors

Many years ago, after the great flood, Noah did not want the animals to leave the ark. He wanted a sign from God that the rains had really stopped. So God moved all the clouds to the edge of the world. The clouds took the curved shape of the sky. Then He shined the sun on the clouds. Soon, there was a beautiful bow of color in the sky. God had created the first rainbow.

Then Noah understood that he could safely open the great doors of the ark. He let everybody out. Of course, all the animals were delighted to be free, but the birds were especially happy. They flew right into the rainbow and through it and back again.

The birds that flew into the blue color became blue; the ones that flew into the red became red. The yellow birds of today are the ones that flew into the yellow. Some of the birds were so excited that they flew around and around in the rainbow. They became multi-colored.

The little hummingbird was very fast and energetic. He flew through the rainbow many times. That is why he has every color of the rainbow on him. To this day, birds have wonderful colors because once, a long time ago, they bathed in God's rainbow.

New Words.

Underline new words in the story. Write them below and find out their meaning.

Write **T** for True and **F** for False.

1. ____ After the flood, Noah did not want the animals

to leave the ark.

2. ____ Noah waited for a sign from God.

3. ____ God created many clouds.

4. ____ He shined the sun on the clouds.

5. ____ God created the first rainbow.

6. ____ The animals did not want to leave the ark.

7. ____ Only the birds left the ark.

8. ____ The birds flew over the rainbow.

9. ____ Some birds flew around and around in the rainbow.

10. ____ The hummingbird has all the colors of the rainbow.

☞ *Check your answers in the story; then write your score here and on page 97.* **Right: ____/10**

Write. Finish these sentences.

After the great flood

So God

The birds

The hummingbird

That is why

Why Birds Are Different Colors

Read, write, and look again.

Many years ago, after the _____ flood, Noah did not want the

animals to leave the ark. He wanted a sign from God that the rains

had _____ stopped. So God moved _____ the clouds to the edge of

the world. The clouds took the _____ shape of the sky. Then He

shined the sun on the clouds. Soon, there was a _____ bow of

color in the sky. God had created the _____ rainbow.

Then Noah understood that he could

_____ open the great doors of the ark.

He let everybody out. Of course, all the

animals were _____ to be _____,

but the birds were especially _____.

They flew right into the rainbow and

through it and back again.

The birds that flew into the blue color became _____; the

ones that flew into the red became red. The yellow birds of today are

the ones that flew into the yellow. Some of the birds were so

_____ that they flew around and around in the rainbow. They

became _____.

The little hummingbird was very _____ and _____. He flew

through the rainbow _____ times. That is why he has _____

color of the rainbow on him. To this day, birds have _____ colors

because once, a _____ time ago, they bathed in God's rainbow.

Pronounce these words.

crashed	moved	wanted
sneaked	curved	created
looked	shined	delighted
rushed	multi-colored	excited
stopped	bathed	
	opened	

Use the words above in these sentences. Then say the sentences.

1. He quietly _____ into the hut.

2. He _____ inside and saw many fish.

3. It _____ to the ground and broke.

4. The water _____ out and covered the earth.

   * * * * * * * * * * * * * * * *

5. All the birds were _____ and _____.

6. Some of the birds became _____.

7. Noah _____ a sign from God.

8. God _____ a rainbow.

9. Finally, the rains _____.

10. The birds _____ in the rainbow.

11. God _____ the clouds.

12. He _____ the sun on the clouds.

13. It was _____ like a bow.

14. Noah _____ the doors to let the animals out.

Why Birds Are Different Colors

Write a sentence for each word.

understand

understood

fly

flew

become

became

safe

safely

happy

happily

color

colorful

multi-colored

Listen to and tell the story of the birds and the rainbow.

Many years ago, after the great flood, ...

He wanted ....

So God moved ....

The clouds ....

Soon, there was ....

Then Noah understood ....

Of course, all the animals ....

They flew ....

The birds that flew ....

The little hummingbird ....

To this day, ...

 ## *Put on a play.*

Tell the story "Why Birds Have Different Colors" as a play.
These are the characters:

Announcer

God

Noah

Bluebird

Redbird

Yellowbird

Hummingbird

How Fire Came to the World

Siberia

Discuss.

Do you know these words?

Creator, fire, apologize, stone, iron

Read.

The Great **Creator** made people. He saw that the earth was very cold and people would die. He knew that people needed **fire**. He came to earth to help the man Ulgen. But Ulgen's daughters laughed at Him. He went away angry. The daughters wanted to **apologize**. They heard Him say "a sharp **stone** and hard **iron**."

Answer.

1. How was the earth?
2. What would happen to the people?
3. What did the people need?
4. What did the Great Creator do?
5. Who laughed at Him?
6. What did He do when they laughed at Him?
7. What did the daughters want to do?

Discuss.

What was the meaning of "a sharp stone and hard iron?"
What did the daughters do when they heard that, and then what happened?

How Fire Came to the World

The Great Creator, Kudai, made the earth and everything on the earth. He created people to live on the earth. But the cold of winter was too strong. When Kudai saw that the man Ulgen was very cold, He said, "I must show him how to start a fire, or he will die."

Kudai appeared on earth to help Ulgen. He came as an old man with a very long beard. Ulgen had three daughters. They saw Kudai. As Kudai started to move, He tripped on His long beard and almost fell. The daughters laughed at Him. This made Kudai angry. He walked away and decided not to tell Ulgen how to start a fire.

Later, the three girls wanted to apologize. They found Kudai sitting on a rock. He was talking to himself. He was still angry so they hid behind a rock and listened. "A sharp stone and hard iron. They will never have fire."

Ulgen's daughters went home. They found their father trying to start a fire with little pieces of wood and a stone. They told him what the old man said.

Ulgen took an iron knife and a stone. He struck them together and there was a spark. When the spark hit the wood, there was fire.

Ulgen's smile was as bright as the fire. Now he and his daughters would be warm. From that time on, there has been fire in the homes of man.

New Words.

Underline new words in the story. Write them below and find out their meaning.

Write T for True and F for False.

1. ____ Kudai was the Great Creator.
2. ____ Ulgen was Kudai's daughter.
3. ____ Ulgen asked Kudai for fire.
4. ____ Kudai came to earth as an old man with a beard.
5. ____ Ulgen's daughters made Kudai angry.
6. ____ The daughters apologized and talked to Kudai.
7. ____ Kudai told them to start a fire with wood and a stone.
8. ____ The daughters told Ulgen to use iron and stone.
9. ____ When Ulgen hit the stone on the wood it made a spark.
10. ____ When the spark hit the wood there was fire.

☞ *Check your answers in the story; then write your score here and on page 97.* **Right: ____/10**

Write. Finish these sentences.

Kudai made

Kudai appeared

The daughters laughed

They found Kudai

They went home and

36

Read, write, and look again.

The _____ Creator, Kudai, made the earth and everything on the earth. He created people to live on the earth. But the _____ of winter was too _____. When Kudai saw that the man Ulgen was very _____, He said, "I must show him how to start a fire, or he will die."

Kudai appeared on earth to help Ulgen. He came as an _____ man with a very _____ beard. Ulgen had three daughters. They saw Kudai. As Kudai started to move, He tripped on his _____ beard and almost fell. The daughters laughed at Him. This made Kudai _____.

He walked _____ and decided not to tell Ulgen how to start a fire.

Later, the three girls wanted to apologize. They found Kudai sitting on a rock. He was talking to Himself. He was still _____ so they hid behind a rock and listened. "A _____ stone and _____ iron. They will _____ have fire."

Ulgen's daughters went home. They found their father trying to start a fire with _____ pieces of wood and a stone. They told him what the old man said.

Ulgen took an _____ knife and a stone. He struck them together and there was a spark. When the spark hit the wood, there was fire.

Ulgen's smile was as _____ as the fire. Now he and his daughters would be _____. From that time on, there has been fire in the homes of man.

Pronounce these words.

years	sticks	dances
skies	feasts	sizes
spears	stripes	pieces
holes	months	surprises

Use nine of the words above in these sentences. Then say the sentences.

1. They used their _____ to touch the sky.

2. He was trying to light the _____ of wood.

3. They were dancing with _____.

4. There were many _____ in the tree.

5. Some animals have many _____.

6. The great flood continued for many _____.

7. The people enjoyed many wonderful _____.

8. There were many different shapes and _____ of fish.

9. After many _____ the people decided to rest.

Write a sentence for each word.

fall

fell

say

said

strike

struck

find

found

hide

hid

tell

told

hit

hit

Listen to and tell the story of how fire came to the world.

The Great Creator, Kudai, made ....

He created ....

But the cold ....

When Kudai saw ....

Kudai appeared ....

Ulgen had three ....

As Kudai started to move, ...

The daughters laughed ....

Later, the three girls ....

He was talking ....

Ulgen's daughters ....

They told him ....

Ulgen took ....

When the spark ....

Now he and his daughters ....

From that time on, ...

 Put on a play.

Tell the story of "How Fire Came to the World" as a play.
These are the characters:

Kudai

Ulgen

Ulgen's daughters

Why the Pheasant Has Red Eyes
A Folktale from Nepal

Discuss.

Do you know these words?

pheasant, chick, fox, prince

Read.

A **pheasant** was very proud of her **chicks**. A **fox** wanted to eat the chicks. The pheasant said he should wait until the chicks were big. The pheasant called the fox a **prince**. The fox was pleased to be called "prince." The pheasant said she would tell everyone to call him a prince. But nobody did. The fox became very angry.

Answer.

1. What was the pheasant proud of?
2. What did the fox want to do?
3. The pheasant told the fox do do what?
4. What did the pheasant call the fox?
5. How did the fox feel?
6. Why did the fox become angry?

Discuss.

When nobody called the fox "prince," he became angry.
What did he do then?

41

Why the Pheasant Has Red Eyes

Once upon a time a pheasant laid several beautiful eggs. When they hatched she was very proud of her eight cute little chicks.

However, a hungry fox found the nest. He was about to eat the chicks when the pheasant cried out, "Oh, great prince of the forest, you should wait until they grow up. Then they will be nice and plump."

The fox decided not to eat the chicks, and he was very pleased to be called prince of the forest. "I am very glad that you called me prince of the forest, but why are you the only one to do that?"

"Oh, great prince," said the pheasant, "I will tell everyone you are our prince. Then everyone will call you that."

As soon as the fox left, the pheasant moved her family and prepared a trap. Meanwhile, day after day, none of the animals called him prince, not even an insect. He became very angry and went to find the pheasant.

At last, he found her sitting on her nest. She was protecting her chicks. But when the fox jumped at her, he fell into a pit that she had prepared. The pheasant flew up to a branch of a tree and began to laugh. As she laughed, the fox tried to get out, but he couldn't. The pheasant laughed and laughed. Tears flowed from her eyes, and her eyes became red.

To this day, the pheasant has red eyes.

New Words.

Underline new words in the story. Write them below and find out their meaning.

*Write **T** for True and **F** for False.*

1. ____ The pheasant laid seven beautiful eggs.

2. ____ She was very proud of her chicks.

3. ____ A fox found the nest and ate the chicks.

4. ____ The pheasant called the fox a princess.

5. ____ When the fox left, the pheasant moved her family.

6. ____ The pheasant prepared a trap for the fox.

7. ____ Everybody called the fox "prince."

8. ____ The fox found the pheasant sitting in a tree.

9. ____ The fox fell into the trap.

10. ____ The pheasant laughed and her eyes became red.

☞ *Check your answers in the story; then write your score here and on page 97.* **Right: ____/10**

Write. Finish these sentences.

Once upon a time

When they hatched

However,

As soon as

Day after day

At last

To this day,

44

Read, write, and look again.

Once upon a time a pheasant laid several _____ eggs. When they hatched she was very _____ of her eight _____ little chicks.

However, a _____ fox found the nest. He was about to eat the chicks when the pheasant cried out, "Oh, great prince of the forest, you should wait until they grow up. Then they will be _____ and _____."

The fox decided not to eat the chicks, and he was very _____ to be called prince of the forest. "I am very _____ that you called me prince of the forest, but why are you the _____ one to do that?"

"Oh, _____ prince," said the pheasant, "I will tell everyone you are our prince. Then everyone will call you that."

As _____ as the fox left, the pheasant moved her family and prepared a trap. Meanwhile, day after day, _____ of the animals called him prince, not even an insect. He became very _____ and went to find the pheasant.

At last, he found her sitting on _____ nest. She was protecting _____ chicks. But when the fox jumped at her, he fell _____ a pit that she had prepared. The pheasant flew _____ to a branch of a tree and began to laugh. As she laughed, the fox tried to get _____, but he couldn't. The pheasant laughed and laughed. Tears flowed _____ her eyes, and her eyes became _____.

To this day, the pheasant has _____ eyes.

Pronounce these words.

chicks	eat	pheasant	great
prince	tree	eggs	laid
pit	pleased	nest	wait
sitting	see	red	eight
will	hear	went	day
little	tears	fell	became

Use some of the words above in these sentences. Then say the sentences.

1. The _____ laid _____ eggs.

2. The fox decided to _____ and _____ the _____ later.

3. The fox was very _____ to be called _____.

4. The fox found the _____ _____ on her _____.

5. The _____ made her eyes _____.

6. The pheasant _____ eight _____.

8. The fox _____ into the _____, and the pheasant flew

   to a branch in the _____.

Write a sentence for each word.

fox

foxes

prince

princes

branch

branches

tear

tears

eye

eyes

family

families

Listen to and tell the story of the pheasant and the fox.

Once upon a time a pheasant ....

When they ....

However, a hungry fox ....

when the pheasant cried out, "..........."

The fox decided ....

"I am very glad ....

"Oh, great prince," ....

As soon as the fox left, ...

Meanwhile, day after day, ...

He became very angry ....

At last, he found ....

But when the fox jumped, ...

The pheasant flew ....

The pheasant laughed ....

Tears flowed ....

To this day, ...

 ## *Put on a play.*

Tell the story "Why the Pheasant Has Red Eyes" as a play.
These are the characters:

Announcer

Pheasant

Fox

Chicks

Insect

48

How the Peacock Got Its Tail

China

Discuss.

Do you know these words?

peacock, tail, monkey, elephant, feather

Read.

A god decided to make the animals more beautiful. He asked the **monkey**, the horse, and the **elephant** if they wanted to be more beautiful. They all said no. The peacock wanted to be more beautiful. The God gave the peacock beautiful **feathers**.

Answer.

1. What did the god decide to do?
2. How many animals did he ask?
3. Who said "no?"
4. Who wanted to be more beautiful?

Discuss.

What happened when the peacock decided to be more beautiful?

How the Peacock Got Its Tail

Many years ago, one of the gods in heaven looked down into a forest filled with animals. "I think I can make their lives happier by making them more beautiful," he said. So he came to earth to help the animals.

First, he asked the monkey, "Are you happy with the way you look? People often look at you and laugh."

"Let them laugh," answered the monkey. "Look how fast I can swing from tree to tree, and I am much better-looking than the horse. Maybe you can help him."

When the god asked the horse if he wanted to be more beautiful, the horse said proudly, "I am already quite handsome. Why don't you ask the elephant?"

The elephant said, "I don't need help. My size and strength make me beautiful." And he pointed to a peacock on the branch of a tree. "He can use some help."

The peacock jumped down from the branch. "If you could make me more beautiful, I would be very happy."

The god smiled with pleasure. "I will give you a tail of long feathers that will spread out to look like colorful jewels. Each feather will end in a brilliant black eye, prettier than the eye of a princess in the palace of the Emperor."

When the god had done what he had promised, the proud peacock spread his wonderful tail for all the animals to see. And so he has done ever since.

New Words.

Underline new words in the story. Write them below and find out their meaning.

Write T for True and F for False.

1. ____ A god decided to make the animals happier by making them stronger.
2. ____ He told the monkey that people often laugh at him.
3. ____ The monkey said he was better-looking than the horse.
4. ____ The horse told the god to ask the elephant.
5. ____ The elephant said the pheasant needed help.
6. ____ The god was pleased when the peacock said he would be very happy to be prettier.
7. ____ The god gave the peacock long, black feathers.
8. ____ The god gave the peacock some beautiful jewels.
9. ____ Each feather ends with a multi-colored eye.
10. ____ The eyes on the feathers of the peacock are prettier than the emperor's palace.

☞ *Check your answers in the story; then write your score here and on page 97.* **Right: ____/10**

Write. Finish these sentences.

One of the gods looked down

First, he asked the monkey

When the god asked the horse

The elephant said,

The peacock jumped down

52

Read, write, and look again.

_____ years ago, one of the gods in heaven looked down into a forest _____ with animals. "I think I can make their lives _____ by making them more _____," he said. So he came to earth to help the animals.

First, he asked the monkey, "Are you _____ with the way you look? People often look at you and laugh."

"Let them laugh," answered the monkey. "Look how _____ I can swing from tree to tree, and I am much _____ than the horse. Maybe you can help him."

When the god asked the horse if he wanted to be more _____, the horse said _____, "I am already quite _____. Why don't you ask the elephant?"

The elephant said, "I don't need help. My size and strength make me _____." And he pointed to a peacock on the branch of a tree. "He can use some help."

The peacock jumped down from the branch. "If you could make me more _____, I would be very _____."

The god smiled with pleasure. "I will give you a tail of _____ feathers that will spread out to look like _____ jewels. Each feather will end in a _____ black eye, _____ than the eye of a princess in the palace of the Emperor."

When the god had done what he had promised, the _____ peacock spread his _____ tail for all the animals to see. And so he has done ever since.

Pronounce these words.

forest	people	said	happy
filled	peacock	help	asked
fast	pointed	strength	branch
feather	pleasure	spread	black
pheasant	pretty	end	palace
elephant	promised	Emperor	animal

Use some of the words above in these sentences. Then say the sentences.

1. The _____ was _____ with animals.

2. The monkey could swing very _____
   from _____ to _____.

3. The _____ didn't need any _____.

4. The god _____ the _____ if they
   wanted to be _____.

5. The peacock _____ his _____ _____s.

6. Each _____ had a _____ eye at the _____.

Write a sentence for each phrase.

will think

thought

will ask

asked

can swing

swung

will smile

smiled

can spread

spread

will look like

looked like

will end

ended

will promise

promised

Listen to and tell the story of the peacock and its tail.

Many years ago, one of the gods ....

So he came to earth ....

First, he asked the monkey, "..........."

"Let them laugh," ....

When the god asked the horse ....

The elephant said, ".........."

And he pointed to a peacock ....

The peacock jumped ....

"If you could make me ....

The god smiled ....

"I will give you ....

Each feather will end in ...."

The proud peacock ....

And so he ....

 Put on a play.

Tell the story of "How the Peacock Got Its Tail" as a play.
These are the characters:

  Announcer

  A god

  Monkey

  Horse

  Elephant

  Peacock

Why There Is Moss On Trees

Eskimo/Inuit from Alaska, U.S.A.

Discuss.

Do you know these words?

moss, seashore, net, hair, noise, needlefish

Read.

Two women were at the **seashore** to catch fish. They caught many fish in their **net**. After they cleaned and cut the fish, they divided them evenly. There was one piece left. They started to fight and pulled each other's **hair**. Then they heard a loud, frightening **noise**. They stopped fighting and got in their boat, and then they heard a **needlefish** make the noise. They were angry at the needlefish, so they ate it. Then they went back to get their fish.

Answer.

1. Why were the women at the seashore?
2. What did they do after they cleaned and cut the fish?
3. What happened when there was one piece left?
4. Why did they stop fighting?
5. What did they hear when they were in the boat?
6. Why did they eat the needlefish?

Discuss.

What happened after they went back to get their fish?

Why There Is Moss On Trees

Long, long ago, two Eskimo women traveled to the seashore every spring. They went to catch fish for the long winter months.

Early one morning they filled their net with fish. Then they cleaned the fish, cut them into thin strips, and hung them in the sun to dry. The two women divided the fish evenly, but there was one piece left over. Each one wanted it. They soon began to fight. They pulled each other's hair so hard that some of it came out and fell on the ground.

Suddenly there was a strange noise. The women were frightened. They stopped fighting, and one of them said, "If it's the forest giant, he will kill us. Let's get out of here."

They ran to the beach and got in their boat. Just then a tiny needlefish opened its mouth wide and made the frightening noise. One of the women snatched up the fish and called it a troublemaker.

The little needlefish answered, "You caused the trouble by fighting. You should be ashamed of yourselves." The angry woman cut it in half, and the two women ate it so it couldn't scold them.

When the women went back to get their fish, they saw hair on the ground. They were so ashamed that they picked it up and threw it into the forest. Ever since then, their hair has been clinging to trees as moss.

New Words.

Underline new words in the story. Write them below and find out their meaning.

Write T for True and F for False.

1. ____ Two Eskimo women went to the seashore every winter.
2. ____ They went to catch fish for the long winter months.
3. ____ When they filled their nets with fish, they began to clean the fish.
4. ____ They put the fish in the sun to dry.
5. ____ They began to fight because they both wanted one more piece of fish.
6. ____ They heard a loud noise that was made by the forest giant.
7. ____ The needlefish made the loud noise.
8. ____ They caught the needlefish.
9. ____ They threw the needlefish into the forest.
10. ____ They were ashamed to see their hair on the ground.

☞ *Check your answers in the story; then write your score here and on page 97.* **Right: ____/10**

Write. Finish these sentences.

Two Eskimo women

They divided the fish

They pulled each other's hair

They ran to the beach

They went back to get their fish

Ever since then

Read, write, and look again.

Long, _____ ago, two Eskimo women traveled to the seashore _____ spring. They went to catch fish for the _____ winter months.

_____ one morning they filled their net with fish. Then they cleaned the fish, cut them into _____ strips, and hung them in the sun to dry, The two women divided the fish _____, but there was one piece _____ _____. Each one wanted it. They soon began to fight. They pulled each other's hair so _____ that some of it came out and fell on the ground.

Suddenly there was a _____ noise. The women were _____. They stopped fighting, and one of them said, "If it's the forest giant, he will kill us. Let's get out of here."

They ran to the beach and got in their boat. Just then a _____ needlefish opened its mouth wide and made the _____ noise. One of the women snatched up the fish and called it a trouble-maker.

The little needlefish answered, "You caused the trouble by fighting. You should be _____ of yourselves." The _____ woman cut it in half, and the two women ate it so it couldn't scold them.

When the women went back to get their fish, they saw hair on the ground. They were so _____ that they picked it up and threw it into the forest. Ever since then, their hair has been clinging to trees as moss.

Pronounce these words.

shore	catch	cleaned	scolded
fish	each	clings	spring
ashamed	snatched	frightening	strange
		ground	trees
			trouble

Use the words above in these sentences. Then say the sentences.

1. They _____ wanted the last piece of _____.

2. They went to the sea_____ every _____

   to _____ _____.

3. When they saw their hair on the _____ they

   were _____.

4. After they _____ the _____ they heard

   a _____ noise.

5. Their hair still _____ to _____.

6. The needle_____ _____ the women and

   told them they caused the _____.

7. The needlefish made a _____ sound.

8. One of the women _____ up the needlefish.

Write a sentence with these words.

Use this pattern:

After they . . . . *(past tense)*,   they. . . . .*(past tense)*

Example:

ask - answer After they asked the question, they answered it.

travel - catch

clean - cut

cut - hang

divide - fight

fight- run

cut - eat

go back - see

pick up - throw

throw - cling

63

Tell the story of the two Eskimo women.

Long, long ago, two Eskimo women ....

They went to catch ....

Early one morning ....

Then they ....

The two women divided ....

They soon began ....

They pulled each other's hair ....

Suddenly ....

They stopped fighting, and ....

They ran to ....

Just then a tiny needlefish ....

One of the women ....

The little needlefish answered, ...

The angry woman cut ....

When the women went back ....

They were so ashamed ....

Ever since then, ...

 Put on a play.

Tell the story "Why There Is Moss on Trees" as a play.
These are the characters:

Announcer

First woman

Second woman

Needlefish

How the Rooster Got
His Red Crown

China

Discuss.

Do you know these words?

rooster, crown, archer, reflection, pool, tiger, roar

Read.

There were six suns in the sky. They were too bright, and they
burned the plants. The Emperor knew his people would die. The
Emperor sent for an **archer** to shoot the suns. The archer saw the
reflections of the suns in a **pool** of water. The archer shot five of the
suns. The sixth sun disappeared behind a hill. Now it was dark in the
morning. A **tiger roared** for the sun, but it did not return. A rooster
crowed. The sun looked to see who made the sound.

Answer.

1. How many suns were in the sky?
2. What did the suns do?
3. What did the Emperor do?
4. Who came to shoot the suns?
5. How many suns did he shoot?
6. What did the sixth sun do?

Discuss.

What happened when the sun returned?

How the Rooster Got His Red Crown

Long, long ago, there were six bright suns in the sky over China. They made the sky too bright and burned the plants below. The Emperor knew that with no plants, his people would die. One of his wise men said, "You should shoot the suns."

So the Emperor sent for a famous archer to shoot down the suns. At first, the archer thought it was impossible, because the suns were too far away. Then he saw their reflections in a pool of water. He shot one reflection and the sun sank to the bottom of the pool. He fired again and again, and soon there were five suns at the bottom of the pool. The sixth sun saw what was happening. He was very frightened, and he disappeared behind a hill.

When everybody woke up the next morning, it was very dark. Now there was no sun. They needed the sun. First, a powerful tiger asked the sun to return. But the tiger's powerful roar only made the sun cover his ears. Many other animals tried to get the sun to return, but they couldn't. Finally, a fat rooster tried. The sun listened. "What a lovely sound," he said, and looked to see who made the sound. When the people saw the sun, they cheered. The sun came out all the way. Then he put a little red crown on the top of the rooster's head.

And every morning since that faraway day, the good rooster wears his red crown and calls for the sun.

New Words.

Underline new words in the story. Write them below and find out their meaning.

Write T for True and F for False.

1. ____ The suns in China burned the plants.
2. ____ The Emperor said, "The only way is to shoot the suns."
3. ____ An archer shot the suns up in the sky.
4. ____ One sun disappeared in a pool.
5. ____ In the morning there were no suns in the sky.
6. ____ A tiger asked the sun to return.
7. ____ The sun did not like the tiger's roar.
8. ____ A rooster asked the sun to return.
9. ____ The sun liked the rooster's sound.
10. ____ The people made a crown for the rooster's head.

☞ *Check your answers in the story; then write your score here and on page 97.* **Right:** ____/10

Write. Finish these sentences.

The six suns in the sky

The Emperor

The archer saw

The sixth sun

Finally, the rooster

The sun

Every morning since that faraway day

68

Read, write, and look again.

Long, _____ ago, there were six _____ suns in the sky over China. They made the sky too _____ and burned the plants below. The Emperor knew that with no plants, his people would die. One of his _____ men said, "You should shoot the suns."

So the Emperor sent for a _____ archer to shoot down the suns. At first, the archer thought it was _____, because the suns were too far _____. Then he saw their reflections in a pool of water. He shot the reflection and the sun sank to the bottom of the pool. He fired again and _____, and soon there were five suns at the bottom of the pool. The sixth sun saw what was happening. He was very _____ and he disappeared behind a hill.

When everybody woke up the _____ morning, it was very _____. Now there was no sun. They needed the sun. First, a _____ tiger asked the sun to return. But the tiger's _____ roar only made the sun cover his ears. Many other animals tried to get the sun to return, but they couldn't. Finally, a _____ rooster tried. The sun listened. "What a _____ sound," he said, and looked to see who made the sound. When the people saw the sun, they cheered. The sun came out _____ the way. Then he put a _____ red crown on the top of the rooster's head.

And _____ morning since that _____ away day, the _____ rooster wears his red crown and calls for the sun.

Pronounce these words.

knew	would	sun
shoot	looked	one
pool	should	what
soon	good	up
rooster	put	cover
you		lovely

Use fourteen of the words above in these sentences. Then say the sentences.

1. The Emperor _____ that the plants and

   people _____die.

2. The archer tried to _____ the _____s.

3. The tiger's roar made the _____ _____ his ears.

4. "_____ a _____ sound," said the sun.

5. _____ of the wise men said, "_____ _____

   _____ the _____s."

6. The _____ _____ now wears a crown.

7. The archer _____ in the _____ and

   saw the suns.

Write sentences with these words.

burned

would burn

died

would die

shot

should shoot

looked

should look

sink

sank

wear

wore

make

made

Tell the story of the rooster and his red crown.

Long, long ago ....

The Emperor knew ....

So the Emperor sent ....

He shot one reflection ....

The sixth sun ....

When everybody woke up ....

First, a powerful tiger ....

Many other animals ....

Finally, a fat rooster ....

"What a lovely sound," ....

Then he put ....

And every morning since ....

 ## *Put on a play.*

Tell the story "How the Rooster Got His Crown" as a play.
These are the characters:

Announcer

Emperor

Wise man

Archer

Sixth sun

Tiger

Rooster

Why Children Are Different Colors

Ghana

Discuss.

Do you know these words?

basket, soil, spirits, model, clay

Read.

The Sky God created earth. He lowered a **basket** with **soil**, plants, and animals to earth. Two **spirits**, a boy and a girl, lived inside the Sky God. They got into the Sky God's mouth to watch the lowering of the basket. The Sky God sneezed and they fell to earth. They felt lonely on earth and decided to make **model** boys and girls. They used **clay** and baked the models in a fire. Then they decided to give the models life.

Answer.

1. What did the Sky God lower to earth?
2. Where did the boy and girl spirits live?
3. What happened when the Sky God sneezed?
4. How did they feel on earth?
5. What did they decide to do?

Discuss.

What happened when the boy and girl spirits made models and gave them life?

73

Why Children Are Different Colors

The Sky God, Nyame, was very clever. He created the sun, moon, and stars by cutting holes in the sky. He filled an enormous basket with soil, plants, and animals and lowered it from the sky to create the earth. Then he noticed an empty space and needed to lower another basket.

Now, Iyaloda was a girl spirit who lived inside Nyame. When she heard that Nyame was lowering another basket, she said to her special boy spirit friend, "Let's watch."

They sneaked up into Nyame's mouth. They climbed over his tongue and leaned out over his lips. Suddenly, Nyame sneezed. The two spirits fell to the earth.

After a while on earth, they began to feel lonely. Iyaloda said, "I have an idea. Let's make little ones like us. We can use clay to make models and bake them in the fire."

So they made boys and girls of clay and baked them. The first models were pale white, creamy white, and pinkish white. The next day they made more, but baked them longer. The models were deep black, dark brown, and reddish brown. Then they made golden yellow and golden brown models.

The boy spirit said, "It is time to breathe life into them." And so, he and Iyaloda became the first father and mother.

And of course, from those first children came all the children of the world, in all their beautiful colors.

New Words.

Underline new words in the story. Write them below and find out their meaning.

Write **T** *for True and* **F** *for False.*

1. ____ The Sky God created the sun.
2. ____ The Sky God cut holes in the sky.
3. ____ Nyame lowered many baskets to earth.
4. ____ He put people in a basket.
5. ____ Iyaloda lived inside Nyame's mouth.
6. ____ The two spirits jumped to earth.
7. ____ They decided to make some other boys and girls.
8. ____ They made the children out of clay.
9. ____ The models were different colors.
10. ____ The boy and girl spirits became the first father and mother.

☞ *Check your answers in the story; then write your score here and on page 97.* **Right:** ____/10

Write. Finish these sentences.

The Sky God

He filled

When she heard

They sneaked

He sneezed

After a while

So they made

76

Why Children Are Different Colors

Read, write, and look again.

The Sky God, Nyame, was very _____. He created the sun, moon, and stars by cutting holes in the sky. He filled an _____ basket with soil, plants, and animals and lowered it from the sky to create the earth. Then he noticed an _____ space and needed to lower _____ basket.

Now, Iyaloda was a girl spirit who lived _____ Nyame. When she heard that Nyame was lowering _____ basket, she said to her _____ boy spirit friend, "Let's watch."

They sneaked up into Nyame's mouth. They climbed over his tongue and leaned out over his lips. _____, Nyame sneezed. The two spirits fell to the earth.

After a while on earth, they began to feel _____. Iyaloda said, "I have an idea. Let's make _____ ones like us. We can use clay to make models and bake them in the fire."

So they made boys and girls of clay and baked them. The first models were _____ white, _____ white, and _____ white. The next day they made more, but baked them _____. The models were _____ black, _____ brown, and _____ brown. Then they made _____ yellow and golden brown models.

The boy spirit said, "It is time to breathe life into them." And so, he and Iyaloda became the _____ father and mother.

And of course, from those _____ children came _____ the children of the world, in _____ their _____ colors.

Pronounce these words.

earth	clever	another	the
heard	lowered	mother	then
first	over	father	that
world	longer	breathed	they
girls			them

Use fifteen of the words above in these sentences. Then say the sentences.

1. _____ Sky God was very _____.

2. He _____ a basket to create _____ _____.

3. _____ made boys and _____.

4. Iyaloda _____ _____ the Sky God was lowering

   _____ basket.

5. They _____ life into _____.

6. They became the _____ _____ and _____.

7. The children of the _____ are now different colors.

Write sentences with these words.

Example: to create — *He decided **to create** the earth*

to lower

to climb

to sneeze

to breathe

to watch

to lean

to bake

to feel

Tell the story "Why Children Are Different Colors."

The Sky God, Nyame, ...

He created ....

He filled ....

Then he noticed ....

Now, Iyaloda was a girl spirit ....

When she heard ....

They sneaked ....

Suddenly, ...

After a while on earth, ...

So they made ....

The first models ....

The boy spirit said, " .... "

And of course, from those first children ....

 Put on a play.

Tell the story "Why Children Are Different Colors" as a play. These are the characters:

Announcer

Nyame

Iyaloda

Boy Spirit

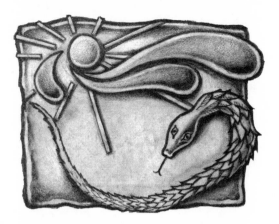

How Men and Women Came to Be

Quiche Maya from Guatemala

Discuss.

Do you know these words?

snake, plains, mountains, valleys, sounds, equals, mist

Read.

Huracan and Feathered **Snake** decided to make earth. They made **plains**, **mountains,** and **valleys**. Then they made plants and animals. They wanted to be thanked. They heard only animal and bird **sounds**. They decided to make men. The men could see the gods, and they thanked them. The gods thought the men would be their **equals**. They decided to blow **mist** in their eyes. Then they made beautiful women and put mist in their eyes.

Answer.

1. Who made the earth and everything in it?
2. What did they want the animals to do?
3. What did they hear?
4. What could the men do?
5. What did the gods do to the men?
6. After they made men, what did they do next?

Discuss.

What happened after the gods put mist in men's and women's eyes?

81

How Men and Women Came to Be

In the beginning, there was a noisy god of the sky named Huracan, and a quiet god named Feathered Snake.

One day the two powerful gods decided to make the earth. Together, they said, "Earth, let it be." Soon there were plains and mountains and valleys. Then they decided to make living things. Together, they said, "Life, let it be." Soon there were plants and animals. There were birds and fish and insects.

The gods wanted to be thanked for their work. Together they said, "Speak. Call our names. Praise us." But all they heard were animal and bird sounds.

Then Huracan said, "We must make man." He and Feathered Snake made four men. The men saw clearly and understood everything. They could see Huracan and Feathered Snake. And — without being asked — they thanked the gods.

The gods were not pleased. "These men are too good," said Feathered Snake. "They will be our equals and stop praising us." Huracan thought for a while. "I will dim their eyes," he said.

He blew a mist into their eyes, and then they could only see things clearly when they were close, and they could not understand and explain everything. When the men were asleep, Huracan and Feathered Snake made four beautiful women. They dimmed their eyes and placed them asleep beside the men.

And so, men and women came to be. Their eyes are still dim, and the world still seems marvelous and mysterious, and so they praise their gods again and again.

New Words.

Underline new words in the story. Write them below and find out their meaning.

Write T for True and F for False.

1. ____ Huracan was a noisy god.
2. ____ The two gods made living things.
3. ____ The animals thanked the gods.
4. ____ The gods made a lot of men.
5. ____ The men saw and understood everything.
6. ____ The men thanked the gods.
7. ____ The gods were very pleased with the men.
8. ____ The gods blew mist into the men's ears.
9. ____ Now men and women see very clearly.
10. ____ They often praise their gods.

☞ *Check your answers in the story; then write your score here and on page 97.* **Right: ____/10**

Write. Finish these sentences.

In the beginning

One day

The Gods wanted

But all they heard

Then Huracan said

He blew

And so,

84

Read, write, and look again.

In the beginning, there was a _____ god of the sky named Huracan, and a _____ god named Feathered Snake.

One day the two _____ gods decided to make the earth. Together, they said, "Earth, let it be." Soon there were plains and mountains and valleys. Then they decided to make _____ things. Together, they said, "Life, let it be." _____ there were plants and animals. There were birds and fish and insects.

The gods wanted to be thanked for their work. Together they said, "Speak. Call _____ names. Praise us." But all they heard were _____ and _____ sounds.

Then Huracan said, "We must make man." He and Feathered Snake made _____ men. The men saw _____ and understood everything. They could see Huracan and Feathered Snake. And — without being asked — they thanked the gods.

The gods were not _____. "These men are too _____," said Feathered Snake. "They will be our equals and stop praising us." Huracan thought for a while. "I will dim their eyes," he said.

He blew a mist into their eyes, and then they could only see things _____ when they were _____, and they could not understand and explain everything. When the men were _____, Huracan and Feathered Snake made four _____ women. They dimmed their eyes and placed them _____ beside the men.

And so, men and women came to be. Their eyes are still _____, and the world still seems _____ and _____, and so they praise their gods again and again.

Pronounce these words.

birds	very	will
begin	valleys	world
baked	live	with
beach	lovely	watch
beside	marvelous	women

Use ten of the words above in these sentences. Then say the sentences.

1. The gods made mountains and _____, and then they made animals and _____.

2. They made four men and four _____.

3. The _____ seems _____ and mysterious.

4. They placed the women _____ the men.

5. They _____ be our equals.

6. The rooster made a _____ sound.

7. The spirits _____ the models.

8. The two _____ fought on the _____ and pulled each other's hair.

Write sentences with these words.

mountain

mountainous

marvel

marvelous

mystery

mysterious

fame

famous

quiet

quietly

clear

clearly

Tell the story of how men and women came to be.

In the beginning, there was a noisy god ....

One day the two powerful gods ....

Then they decided to ....

The gods wanted to be thanked ....

Then Huracan said, "We must make man. ....

They could see Huracan and Feathered Snake ....

The gods were not pleased ....

Huracan thought for a while ....

He blew a mist into their eyes ....

When the men were asleep, ...

And so, ...

 Put on a play.

Tell the story "How Men and Women Came to Be" as a play.
These are the characters:

Announcer

Huracan

Feathered Snake

Man

Woman

Why the Jellyfish Has No Bones

Japan

Discuss.

Do you know these words?

jellyfish, palace, octopus, jealous, medicine, liver

Read.

Long ago the **jellyfish** lived in the **palace** of the Dragon King. He had bones and could swim very fast. Everybody loved the jellyfish. The **octopus** was **jealous**. The daughter of the Dragon King became sick. The octopus said she would die. She needed **medicine** from the **liver** of a monkey. He told the king to send the jellyfish to get a monkey. The jellyfish found a monkey, but the monkey got away. The jellyfish came back to the palace. The octopus beat the jellyfish and broke all his bones.

Answer.

1. Where did the jellyfish live?
2. Who was jealous of the jellyfish?
3. Who became sick?
4. What did the octopus tell the king?
5. Did the jellyfish get the medicine?
6. What happened when the jellyfish returned to the palace?

Discuss.

What happened after the octopus beat the jellyfish?

Why the Jellyfish Has No Bones

Long ago, all the sea creatures lived in the palace of the Dragon King, at the bottom of the sea. In those days, the jellyfish had bones and could swim very fast. All the other fish loved him because he was so kind. But the palace doctor, the octopus, was jealous.

One day, the daughter of the Dragon King became sick. The octopus saw a chance to hurt the jellyfish, and so he lied. He told the king she would certainly die without the medicine made from the liver of a monkey. He asked the king to send the jellyfish to find a monkey.

The jellyfish swam and swam. Finally, he saw a monkey who had fallen into the water. The monkey could not swim, and the kind jellyfish took him on his back. The thankful monkey promised to help the princess.

When they were near the palace, the monkey changed his mind. He said, "I left my liver in a tree on the island. Take me back, and I'll get it." But as soon as the monkey climbed the tree, he waved goodbye. The poor jellyfish swam back to the palace empty-handed.

At the palace the octopus said to the king, "Let me beat this no-good jellyfish for you." And he beat the jellyfish until all its bones were broken. Just then, the princess came in. "I'm all better," she said. Then the king realized that the octopus had lied. He told him to go away and never come back.

And so, the jellyfish became the Dragon King's favorite. And even though he still has no bones and can't swim, the other creatures of the sea do not bother him.

New Words.

Underline new words in the story. Write them below and find out their meaning.

Write T for True and F for False.

1. ____ The Dragon King's palace was on an island.
2. ____ All the fish lived in the palace.
3. ____ Everybody loved the jellyfish.
4. ____ When the king's daughter became sick, the octopus told the jellyfish to find some medicine.
5. ____ The jellyfish didn't find a monkey.
6. ____ At the palace, the king beat the jellyfish.
7. ____ All the jellyfish's bones were broken.
8. ____ The king's daughter didn't die.
9. ____ The king realized the octopus had lied and beat him.
10. ____ The jellyfish became the king's daughter's favorite.

☞ *Check your answers in the story; then write your score here and on page 97.* **Right:** ____/10

Write. Finish these sentences.

Long ago

One day

The jellyfish swam

Finally

When they were near the palace

At the palace, the octupus said to the king

And so, the jellyfish

Read, write, and look again.

_____ ago, all the sea creatures lived in the palace of the Dragon King, at the bottom of the sea. In those days, the jellyfish had bones and could swim very _____. All the other fish loved him because he was so _____. But the palace doctor, the octopus, was _____.

One day, the daughter of the Dragon King became _____. The octopus saw a chance to hurt the jellyfish, and so he lied. He told the king she would _____ die without the medicine made from the liver of a monkey. He asked the king to send the jellyfish to find a monkey.

The jellyfish swam and swam. _____, he saw a monkey who had fallen into the water. The monkey could not swim, and the _____ jellyfish took him on his back. The _____ monkey promised to help the princess.

When they were _____ the palace, the monkey changed his mind. He said, "I left my liver in a tree on the island. Take me back, and I'll get it." But as soon as the monkey climbed the tree, he waved goodbye. The _____ jellyfish swam back to the palace _____.

At the palace the octopus said to the king, "Let me beat this _____ jellyfish for you." And he beat the jellyfish until all its bones were _____. Just then, the princess came in. "I'm all _____," she said. Then the king realized that the octopus had lied. He told him to go _____ and never come back.

And so, the jellyfish became the Dragon King's _____. And even though he still has no bones and can't swim, the _____ creatures of the sea do not bother him.

Pronounce these words.

lived	lie/lied	palace	fallen
loved	long	jellyfish	told
left	liver	jealous	all
look		finally	

Use the words above in these sentences. Then say the sentences.

1. The octopus was _____ of the _____.

2. _____ ago, the creatures _____ in the _____ of the king.

3. All the fish _____ the jellyfish.

4. The octopus _____ to the king.

5. The king sent the jellyfish to _____ for the _____ of a monkey.

6. The monkey said he _____ his _____ in a tree

7. _____ the jellyfish's bones were broken.

8. _____ the jellyfish found a monkey that had _____ into the water.

9. The octopus _____ a _____.

Write sentences with these words.

Example: will beat   *The octopus will beat the jellyfish.*

beat   *The octopus beat the jellyfish.*

had beaten   *After the octopus had beaten the jellyfish,*
the king sent him away.

lie

lied

had lied

swim

swam

had swum

tell

told

had told

Tell the story of the jellyfish and the octopus.

Long ago, all the sea creatures ....

In those days, the jellyfish ....

But the palace doctor, ...

One day, the daughter ....

The octopus saw a chance ....

He told the king ....

The jellyfish swam ....

Finally, he saw a monkey ....

The thankful monkey ....

When they were near the palace, ...

But as soon as the monkey ....

At the palace the octopus said to the king, "..............

And he beat the jellyfish ....

Just then, the princess ....

Then the king realized ....

And so, the jellyfish became ....

 Put on a play.

Tell the story "Why the Jellyfish Has No Bones" as a play.
These are the characters:

Announcer

Jellyfish

Octopus

Dragon King

Monkey

King's daughter

96

☞ *Comprehension Scores* ☜

The Sources of the Stories
and links to related internet sites

Why the Sky Is High
Once in the First Times
Elizabeth Hough Sechrist
Macrae Smith Co., Phila., 1949
www.seasite.niu.edu/Tagalog/folktales/ Tagalog/
    why_the_sky_is_high.htm *(a different tale)*
www.chipublib.org/003cpl/diversity/apahm02/
    fairy_bib/fairytales.html *(other collections)*

How the Chipmunk Got Her Stripes
How People Sang the Mountains Up
Maria Leach, Viking Press, 1967
www.y-indianguides.com/
    pm_st_iroquois_legend.html
www.joysofthespirit.com/Joys.Pages/
    Joys.PagesLegends/chipmunkstripes.html

How the Sea Was Born
*Golden Tales: Myths, Legends and
Folktales from Latin America*
Lulu Delacre, Scholastic Press, 1996
www.hartford-hwp.com/Taino/docs/myths.html
www.cubaheritage.com/
    subs.asp?sID=76&cID=5
http://members.dandy.net/~orocobix/faq2.html

Why Birds Are Different Colors
How People Sang the Mountains Up
Maria Leach, Viking Press, 1967
www.humboldt.edu/~teg1/syllabus/406/students/
    fall97/5/amy.html
www.yale.edu/ynhti/curriculum/units/1993/2/
    93.02.08.x.html
www.prolinguaassociates.com/Pages/
    powbook.html

How Fire Came to the World
Beginnings: Creation Myths of the World
Margaret McElderry, Penelope Farmer
Atheneum, 1979
www.sacred-texts.com/asia/tes/tes04.htm
www.sacred-texts.com/asia/tes/tes33.htm

Why the Pheasant Has Red Eyes
Tales of Kathmandu
Karna Sakya, Linda Griffith
House of Kathmandu,Brisbane, Australia, 1980
http://teacher.scholastic.com/writewit/mff/
    myths_readsch.asp?Age=5
www.pilgrimsbooks.com/folklore.html#
    anchor1109642

How the Peacock Got Its Tail
*The Magic Boat and other Chinese
Folk Stories*
MA Jagendorf, Virginia Weng
Vanguard Press, 1980
www.pitt.edu/~dash/china.htm
www.khasi.ws/peacock.htm

Why There Is Moss on Trees
*Tales of Ticasuk: Eskimo Legends
and Stories*
Emily Ivanoff Brown "Ticasuk"
University of Alaska Press, 1987
www.alaska.edu/opa/eInfo/index.xml?
    StoryID=203
www.americanfolklore.net/folktales/ak.html

How Rooster Got His Red Crown
*Favorite Children's Stories from China
and Tibet*
Lotta Carswell Hume
Charles E. Tuttle, Rutland, Vt.
Copyright © in Japan, 1962
www.pilgrimsbooks.com/folklore.html#
    anchor1109859
www.unc.edu/~rwilkers/frames-china.htm

Why Children Are Different Colors
When the World Was Young
Margaret Mayo
Simon amd Schuster, 1995
www.lehigh.edu/~tqr0/ghanaweb/folktales.html
www.peacecorps.gov/wws/students/folktales/
www.canteach.ca/elementary/africa.html
www.darsie.net/talesofwonder/africa.html

How Men and Women Came to Be
When the World Was Young
Margaret Mayo
Simon and Schuster, 1995
www.jaguar-sun.com/gods.html
www.geocities.com/athens/academy/7286/
    popolvuhmain.html#anchor307278

Why the Jellyfish Has No Bones
Japanese Children's Favorite Stories
Edited by Florence Sakade
Charles E. Tuttle, 1958
www.kuroshio.co.jp/rotaract/fish.html
www.theSereneDragon.net/Tales/
    Japan-jellyfish.html
www.pitt.edu/~dash/japan.html

User's Guide

This fascinating collection of stories is, of course, the "feature attraction" that you and your class will read, write about, listen to, and talk about. Each story is explored and enjoyed in a variety of ways, and in the process of doing that, the participants will sharpen their English language skills.

As explained in the introduction on page v, the stories are sequenced from shorter and easier to longer and more challenging. Therefore, it is best to begin with the very first story and proceed in order to the last story.

There are several activities in each unit. In general, it is best to proceed through the activities in order, especially the first five activities that lead up to and include the complete story. The activities are described below in greater detail.

Title.

The title of each story should be briefly discussed and explained.

Origin.

Take time to look at a map and locate the countries that are represented in the stories. A map is provided on page vi, but a wall map of the world gives more information.

Discuss.

Most of the words in this list are nouns that are central to understanding the story. Give the students the first opportunity to share what they know and don't know. Help them with the definitions and initial explorations of the story. You may also want to introduce the plural forms of the nouns.

Read.

This short reading introduces the story. The sentences are short and simple, and the essential story line is told without detail. However, the story is purposefully not complete.

Answer.

This is simply a quick comprehension check which can be done in different ways: 1) the teacher poses the questions and individuals respond, 2) individuals do a silent self-check, 3) pairs or small groups check each other orally. Answering the questions successfully indicates that the students have understood the introductory reading and are ready to take on the complete reading.

Discuss.

This question asks the students to use their own imaginations to complete the story. This discussion is best done in small groups to allow for differences in interpretation and expresssion.

Illustration.

Talk about the full-page illustration. A leading question can be: "What's happening here?" This establishes the context, and that will make the comprehension of the story and subsequent learning more effective.

Read.

Have the students read the complete stories individually. As indicated previously, the stories increase in length and lexical and grammatical complexity. After the first, each successive story builds on the previous ones to encourage a feeling of success and progress. As the students read, the teacher can circulate to help individuals who are having difficulty. However, the students should be encouraged to try to read through the complete story without stopping at each troublesome word. They should develop the habit of trying to comprehend the unknown elements by examining the context.

New Words.

It is impossible to predict with complete accuracy which words in the story will give the students trouble. Therefore, there should be an opportunity for the students to note their own troublesome words. They should do this immediately after finishing the reading, and time should be allowed to understand these words. After the students have made their lists, they can compare them in pairs or small groups. After they have helped each other, the teacher can help with examples and definitions of the words that are most troublesome.

Write T for True and F for False.

This is a simple true-false comprehension check. The students can record their scores in the back of the book and note their progress as they proceed through the stories. The answers are available in the story, and so by looking at the story again the students will improve their comprehension.

Write. Finish these sentences.

This short writing practice also results in a synopsis of the story.

Read, write, and look again.

This activity focuses on adjectives, adverbs, and an occasional preposition. It can be done as a dictation, or as a gapped passage that requires the students to pay attention to modifying words.

Pronounce these words.

This activity focuses on a variety of pronunciation problems. A useful procedure is for the teacher to model the pronunciation, and then have the class and finally, individuals say the words. For a listing of the specific pronunciation features, see page 104.

Use the words above in these sentences. Then say the sentences.

Finding the right word for the gap is an exercise in knowing the meaning of the words featured in the pronunciation exercise. Pairs of students can check each other's answers. Saying the sentence is an opportunity to practice the stress-timed rhythm of spoken English. The content words get the heaviest stress (long and loud) while the function words usually get weak stress. For example, the students should say (from "Why the Sky is High"):

No_{body} need_{ed to} work.

_{The} spear stabbed _{the} sky

_{They} danced _{at the} feast.

One simple way to do this is to say the sentence with its natural rhythm, and then have the class say it in unison as you clap or tap the rhythm.

Write a sentence with these words.

This activity focuses on a grammatical or lexical feature. Special emphasis is given to verb forms and tenses. You may want to have the students do this first on a separate piece of paper to be handed in to you. This allows you to check the accuracy of their sentences, hand the papers back, and have the students write the correct (and corrected) sentences in the book.

Listen to and tell the story.

This can be done as a dictation activity, a storytelling activity, or both. One way to do this activity, is to have students follow along in their books as you read the original, complete story. The students can fill in the empty spaces with words and phrases as you dictate. Then you can have the students work in pairs, and practice telling the story to each other. They can use the partial text in the beginning and then as they become more confident, they can try telling the story from memory (not necessarily verbatim, of course).

Put on a play.

This final activity can be omitted if it seems inappropriate for your class. However, it affords a great opportunity for the students to put to use some of the words and phrases they have encountered in the story. This can be done with a written script or simply as a kind of skit.

Pronunciation Problems

Why the Sky Is High
    Regular past tense endings: /t/   /d/   /id/

How the Chipmunk Got Her Stripes
    Regular past tense endings: /t/   /d/   /id/

How the Sea Was Born
    Regular past tense endings: /t/   /d/   /id/

Why Birds Are Different Colors
    Regular past tense endings: /t/   /d/   /id/

How Fire Came to the World
    Plural "s":   /s/   /z/   /iz/

Why the Pheasant Has Red Eyes
    Vowel contrasts: /i/—/iy/   and   /e/—/ey/

How the Peacock Got Its Tail
    Consonant contrast: /f/ — /p/,
    Vowel contrast: /e/ — /æ/

Why There Is Moss on Trees
    Consonant contrast: /sh/ — /ch/
    Consonant clusters

How the Rooster Got His Red Crown
    Vowel contrasts: /uw/ — /u/ — /√/

Why Children Are Different Colors
    /ər/ and /ð/

How Men and Women Came To Be
    Consonant contrasts: /b/ — /v/ — /w/

Why the Jellyfish Has No Bones
    Consonant: / l /

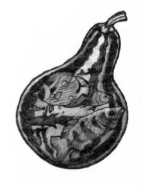

Grammatical and Lexical Features

Why the Sky Is High
  Irregular verbs, present and past tense

How the Chipmunk Got Her Stripes
  Irregular verbs, present and past tense

How the Sea Was Born
  Irregular verbs, present and past tense

Why Birds Are Different Colors
  Irregular verbs, adjective-adverb forms

How Fire Came to the World
  Irregular verbs, present and past tense

Why the Pheasant Has Red Eyes
  Singular and plural nouns

How the Peacock Got Its Tail
  Modal + verb and past tense

Why There Is Moss on Trees
  Past tense

How the Rooster Got His Red Crown
  Modal + verb and past tense

Why Children Are Different Colors
  Infinitives

How Men and Women Came To Be
  Noun-adjective/adverb forms

Why the Jellyfish Has No Bones
  Present, future, past perfect

Other Publications from Pro Lingua

The art of storytelling is an excellent way to involve your students in speaking effectively and listening critically. The stories in the first three collections can be cut from the books and used as story card prompts. Students read the brief tales, put the cards down, and tell their stories from memory.

- **Nasreddin Hodja: Stories to Read and Retell.** Hodja (the teacher) has been a favorite folk hero in his native Turkey and throughout the Islamic world for 800 years. These droll stories are short and fun to tell, and they appeal to people from all cultures. The book can be enjoyed as a reader, or each page can be removed from the book and used to stimulate storytelling.

- **Story Cards: North American Indian Tales**. 48 animal stories collected from tribes across North America. The tales explain how the world came to be as it is (How Porcupine Got Her Quills, etc.) Each story is on a separate story card with a colorful illustration by Rainbow Cougar, a popular Native American artist.

- **Story Cards: Aesop's Fables**. This collection of stories features 48 of Aesop's classic stories, many of them known the world over. Each story is on a separate story card with a colorful and charming illustration.

- **Pearls of Wisdom** is a collection of 12 African and Caribbean folktales for listening and reading. Dr. Raouf Mama, a West African griot (storyteller) who collected these tales, reads them dramatically for listening practice. Along with the **text** and the two **cassettes,** a **student workbook** contains exercises in critical thinking, discussion, and writing, vocabulary, and other skill areas.

- **Plays for the Holidays. Historical and Cultural Celebrations.** Students begin with a reading and exercises introducing each of the major U.S. holidays. Then they put on a brief play as a way of participating in the holiday. Most of the plays are based on American history.

- **Celebrating American Heroes. The Playbook** is a collection of 13 short plays featuring an interesting group of heroes, from the very famous (Lincoln, Washington, Edison) to the less well-known (Dolley Madison, Jonas Salk, John Muir, Cesar Chavez, Harriet Beecher Stowe). The format of the plays is similar to that of *Plays for the Holidays,* with a few leading characters, a narrator, and a chorus. The **photocopyable Teacher's Guide** includes several pronunciation and vocabulary worksheets. The plays are also available on a **cassette recording.**

- **Heroes from American History.** An integrated skills content-based **reader** for intermediate ESL. All the heroes in the playbook (above) are featured as well as Maya Lin, Eleanor Roosevelt, and the "ordinary citizen." There are maps and timelines that bring out the historical context of the times when these heroes lived.